Protected by My Roommate

Cameron Hart

Published by Cameron Hart, 2024.

PROTECTED BY MY ROOMMATE

First edition. June 27, 2024.

ISBN: 979-8227092410

Written by Cameron Hart.

Want a free book?

Sign up for my newsletter[1] and get your free copy of Chasing Stacy!

One look at the stunning waitress carrying the weight of the world on her shoulders, and I'm a goner. I wasn't looking for a sweet little thing with auburn hair and more baggage than I can fit on the back of my bike, but there's no going back now. She's mine. I'll prove to her I'm more than capable of handling her past and making her feel safe again.

---

1. https://dl.bookfunnel.com/7wbqvhsx8r

Chapter 1

Delaney

"Delaney, can you clear off table twelve before you clock out?"

I check my watch, then nod at my coworker before heading over to the corner table. It's the end of a long overnight shift at Ron's Diner, and I need to make sure I'm out the door by five-thirty. That way I can get home by six, before my brothers wake up.

It's risky, sneaking out several nights a week to wait tables at Ron's, but I don't have much of a choice if I want to escape my controlling brothers. I'm the youngest of four and the only girl. I never knew my mom, but I was reminded over and over that her passing was my fault. She died while giving birth to me.

My father was in over his head with four kids, so we were left to our own devices most of the time. He ended up getting into some trouble with a big crime family here in New York, the Romanos, and they silenced him the only way they could - a bullet to the head and a grave at the bottom of the Hudson River.

That was ten years ago. I was just twelve at the time. Most pre-teens are obsessed with bands, crushes, movies, and fashion. Me? I just wanted safety. A place to hide. I still do. I know all too well that monsters are real. Only, they don't live under your bed. They walk the streets, in broad daylight, confident that they can get away with anything. And for the most part, they do.

That's why I need to get out. My brothers have started working for the same crime family that killed our father, and it's only a matter of time before that lifestyle gets all of us killed.

I shake my head, trying to clear the unpleasant thoughts. It never works, but at least I'm trying. I return my focus to the task at hand, stacking the dirty plates into the dish tub, followed by cups and silverware.

Carrying everything to the back room, I set the tub down and begin rinsing the dishes and placing them in the dishwasher. I check my watch again, scrambling to the employee lockers to grab my things. I pull on black sweatpants and a giant black hoodie, along with a black stocking cap. Shoving my tips into the front pocket of my black backpack, I rush to the time clock next to the back door and enter my employee number before hitting the clock out button.

Dang it. It's five thirty-five, which means I missed my bus.

Sure enough, as soon as I burst through the back door and jog down the alleyway, I see my bus pull away from the stop. My shoulders drop and my stomach ties itself in knots. I trudge to the bus stop and read the schedule posted next to the sign. The next bus won't be here for another thirty minutes.

Tears burn the back of my eyes, but I blink them away and take a deep breath. Crying won't rewind time, so all I can do is move forward and figure out something else. Truthfully though... I'm so damn tired. Every single day is a battle to get up and go through the motions. I have to believe it's all building toward something. My freedom, hopefully. If my brothers don't kill me for sneaking out and getting a job without them knowing, that is.

I check my phone to see if there are any ride shares available but, of course, it's too early for most people to be out and about. Looking up from my screen, I scan the street until my eye catches on a yellow taxi cab.

I hesitate for a moment but then flag the driver down. He sees me and pulls over to the side while I shuffle through my backpack to get my tip money. I know this one ride will cost at least half of my tips, but I'm trying not to think about it. I don't have a choice. I'd rather be short on tip money than risk the wrath of my brothers.

After my dad died, my brothers raised me, if you could call it that. More like ordered me around and treated me like a servant. When I wasn't cooking or cleaning, I was up in my room.

At first, it was because I was told to be neither seen nor heard unless I was helping out around the house. But I grew to love my afternoons and evenings by myself. I read anything I could get my hands on. When I discovered that I could rent books from the library for free, my whole world opened up.

I learned about bird calls, the deep ocean, mighty dragons, and daring princes. I read books about stars and galaxies, chemistry, and the inspiring lives of great explorers and philosophers. I found a thousand different ways of life between the pages of my beloved books, and it only made me hungry to break free and start my own.

"Where to?" the cab driver asks, startling me from my thoughts.

I give him the address of the convenience store a few blocks from my house. I don't want him to drop me off out front in case the lights or the sound of the engine wakes my brothers.

We ride in silence, and I look out the window, watching the sun turn from pink to orange to yellow, covering the city in warm light. The landscape changes from skyscrapers to strip malls and, eventually, the cab comes to a stop in front of a 7-Eleven.

"You know this place doesn't open until seven, right? It's right there in the name, babe," the driver says.

My eyes dart to his in the rearview mirror. I notice for the first time he has a creepy smile, full of yellow teeth. A chill runs down my spine, but I ignore it. I've been in worse places with more dangerous people than this cabbie.

I shrug my shoulders and hand him my fare plus a tip. I may not appreciate the vibe this guy is giving off, but I know what it's like to live off tips and save every penny. I always try to give a little extra whenever I can.

He takes the cash, and I step out of the cab, grabbing my backpack and slinging it over my shoulder. I trudge up the slight hill toward the only home I've ever known. It's not in a great neighborhood, but it's not the worst one, either. I've tried keeping up on house repairs over the years, but I stopped growing at five feet and two inches, so I've been limited on what projects I can do without help.

Still, a smile pulls at my lips as I see the two-story house nestled between apartment buildings. I planted flowers out front last week, and they're in full bloom. Tim, my eldest brother, made fun of me for trying to make our "shithole house" look presentable. His words, not mine.

But I don't care. They aren't for him. They're for me. A little bright spot in my day. I can look out my window in the morning and see a pop of color, reminding me that all sorts of beautiful things can grow in unexpected places.

As I approach the little house, I notice an unfamiliar car parked across the street. It could be someone visiting a friend in one of the apartment buildings nearby, but it wasn't here when I left for work at ten last night.

My muscles tense as my heart picks up speed. Awareness prickles my skin, making the hair on the back of my neck stand up. As I get closer, I notice the car is a sleek black BMW. Not the kind of car that frequents this side of the tracks.

I clench my jaw, trying to calm myself with a deep breath. It's not working. The last time a luxury vehicle was parked outside my house, it left with my father's body stuffed in the trunk.

I only have a few moments to decide what to do. Did my brothers wake up and notice I was gone? Did they call in a favor with the Romanos to track me down? Tim is the earliest riser, but he's normally still half asleep at seven when I'm up and making coffee for everyone. I can't imagine anyone checking on me, either.

So who is here? And why?

I consider making a run for it, but then remember I only have a few dollars left of my tip money. Everything else is stashed in my room. If I can sneak upstairs and grab it, I could go somewhere else for a few days, rent a cheap motel in cash and work on a plan to disappear. Sure, it's way ahead of schedule, but I have to try.

I make my way around to the side of the house and peer through the kitchen window. There's a light on in the living room, and I can see the animated shadow of someone throwing their hands up. I hold my breath, listening for a few moments.

Tim's deep voice grunts something, followed by my middle brother, Derek. Patrick, the youngest of my brothers, speaks up, his voice higher and more excited than the previous two.

Good. All three of my brothers are in the living room. That should make it easier to sneak in if they're all in one place.

I pry the kitchen window open an inch at a time, waiting until someone talks or laughs to cover the sound. Usually, I just walk through the back door after my shift at the diner but, occasionally, I've had to improvise. Once the window is open enough for me to slip through, I locate the large stepping stone I found months ago and move it in place.

Hoisting myself up, I wiggle through the opening, cursing my wide hips and the extra junk in my trunk. I guess it's been a while since I've had to use the window. I don't remember it being this difficult to wedge myself...

"What is this?" a gruff, thickly accented voice asks from somewhere behind me. "A little piggy breaking in?"

My eyes go wide, and I try to scramble through the window to escape the stranger. He wraps a hand around my calf and pulls. Hard. I grip the window sill, biting back a scream as the metal edge cuts into my palms.

"You are the sister, yes?" The man tugs me away from the window, then gathers my wrists in one of his large hands, holding them behind my back. "Let's go inside and talk to your brothers. We've been waiting for you."

I look at the man over my shoulder, then snap my eyes forward. He's pure evil. I can see it. Feel it. The black in his eyes matches the sickness in his heart.

"W-waiting?" I stutter. My head is spinning and it feels like I'm breathing through a straw.

"Yes, little piggy."

I open my mouth to ask what the hell he's talking about, but he lets go of my wrists, grabbing my bicep instead. His fingers squeeze my flesh painfully as he pushes me down into an empty chair.

My vision blurs and my stomach twists in on itself as I look around the room. Tim, Patrick, and Derek are sitting on the couch, and a large man in a fancy suit and salt-and-pepper hair sits in a recliner across from them. Four pairs of eyes land on me, and without looking, I know the other man standing behind me is focused on me as well.

Tim is the first to speak. "Dear sister," he starts, leaning forward so his elbows are on his knees. "Did you think we didn't notice you sneaking out at night?"

I wince at his sickly-sweet tone, feeling myself deflate at his words. My chest grows tight and my heart hammers a hole through my ribcage.

Tim smirks at me, his hazel eyes glinting with malice. "Thanks for the extra cash, by the way. We found your stash a while ago, and just cleared the last of it out when you left for your shift earlier tonight. I figured if you want to help out financially, there's an easier way to do it."

"What are you–"

"Ah, ah, Delaney. Not your turn to speak. I've struck a deal with our good friend, Angelo Romano."

Romano. I was right. This situation is getting worse by the second.

The man with salt-and-pepper hair, Angelo, I assume, grunts as he eyes me up and down. I recoil from his gaze, only to be jerked up by the guy gripping my arm.

"Bring her here," Angelo says, pointing to a spot right in front of him.

I'm dragged across the room and positioned in front of the large, intimidating man. He grips my jaw and jerks my head right and left, making my neck hurt. His eyes roam up and down my body, making my stomach twist in fear. I swallow down bile and try to take a step back. The hand on my arm tightens, making me whimper.

"She's pretty, this is true. But she's too… round. Too chubby," he states bluntly.

I've never been happier to be called fat. Does that mean he doesn't want me? I'm no genius, but I've connected the dots here. Apparently, my brothers thought it was a great idea to sell me to the Romanos, or at least give me to the Romanos so they can sell me.

I can't process that betrayal right now. The sad part is, I'm not even that surprised.

"Put her on a diet," Tim pipes up.

"Excuse me?" I cut a glance at my eldest brother, still not able to wrap my head around what is happening.

"And she's young. Too young," Angelo continues.

Both men talk over each other about me, as if I'm not even here. I suppose in their world, women are merely ornamental.

"She's a good cook. And always keeps our place clean. If you don't want to use her for, uh…" Patrick trails off, clearing his throat as he lets the unfinished sentence hang in the air. "I'm just saying, she can be a housekeeper or a yard worker or–"

"Enough!" Angelo bellows.

The room grows deathly silent. Blood rushes through my ears, my heart beating a staccato rhythm against my chest. *What the actual fuck is happening right now? Am I really being sold to the mafia?*

"Sir," the man who grabbed me from the window whispers as he leans in closer to Angelo. "Their debt is upwards of a million. Do you think *she* is worth that kind of cash?" He doesn't even try to hide his disdain for me as his beady little black eyes roam up and down my body.

Angelo leans back in the chair, scratching his chin as he looks me over. "No," he states simply. The large man scoffs and waves his hand in the air, dismissing me.

Oh, thank all the gods I can think of!

I pull my arm from the man's death grip and rub the sore spot on my upper arm.

"This is not what you promised me. She's no good," Angelo says with a hard look directed at Tim.

"What?" Tim exclaims, standing up from his position on the couch. "You said if we brought you a promising business opportunity, our debt would be forgiven."

"And what business opportunity did you have in mind?" Angelo asks.

"Well, you traffic guns, right?" Derek answers after a beat of silence. "We figured you probably trafficked women, too."

Angelo slowly rises from his seat, his barrel chest and protruding stomach seemingly taking up the whole room. When he crosses his arms and stares at my brothers, I want to duck under the kitchen table and take cover.

"Despicable. All of you. We don't traffic women or children. Besides, giving up your sister because she's an easy target? That's not the work ethic, nor the morality I want from my men."

"Morality? Fucking *morality*?" Tim shouts. "That's rich, coming from a goddamn mafia captain."

"Exactly," Angelo snaps. "So how much of a piece of shit does that make you?"

Tim glares at the man before glancing at Patrick and Derek still seated on the couch. Tim rolls his eyes and squares his shoulders, ready to face Angelo again. "Fine. Give me a week and we'll think of something else."

"Not so fast," Angelo replies. He looks over at his partner in crime, and the two of them whisper Italian back and forth until the goon nods his head and wanders away.

"Where is he going?" Tim asks.

"Do not worry about him. You have a debt. And now you've dragged your sister into it. While I don't delight in shedding innocent blood, I can't have loose ends."

"What?" I gasp, instinctively backing away.

My captor grabs my wrist and tugs me forcefully against him before shoving me into Tim. My brother seethes, his hazel eyes full of rage and disgust.

"Shut her up. Then, I'll be back to collect. The full amount, in cash, by next week. You won't like the consequences if you're late again."

A whimper escapes my lips, despite my best efforts to keep my panic attack at bay.

"You mean, kill her?" Derek looks a little appalled by the idea.

Hope blooms in my chest. Maybe he'll help me escape.

Angelo's eyes narrow. "You had no problem selling her, so what difference does it make?"

A tense silence fills the room. One wrong word and this could turn into a bloody crime scene. I've seen it happen before, all those years ago.

"Fine," Tim states finally.

Patrick and Derek stiffen, then nod, accepting their part in all this.

I'm still in shock as I watch Angelo and his goon file out the front door. Tim is right behind them, chattering away about timing and business plans. Patrick and Derek are on their phones, probably trying to scrape up money with a few internet cons.

Now, my brain shouts. *Leave now, while no one is looking.*

Sweat beads my forehead and upper lip, and the cuts on my palms sting as I clench my fists. My eyes dart to the door, then back to the couch as I slowly back away. Every muscle in my body is trembling, and I can barely hear my thoughts over the *thud-thud-thud* of my poor heart.

I calculate how many steps it would take me to get to the back door. About fifteen. I can do that. I can make it out the back door.

Then what?

My feet are on the run before I can think it all the way through. I pivot on my right foot, then focus on the door with each step. My fingers wrap around the doorknob. I'm so close I can feel the cool night air blowing in through the crack under the door.

A hand clamps down on my shoulder, and I'm ripped backward, tripping on my feet and tumbling to the ground. I hit the floor so hard, the breath is knocked from my lungs.

I'm frozen in place, laying on my back, trying to gasp for air. Tim towers over me, his eyes narrowing in disgust.

"P-please..." I choke. "I'll go. I'll go and never come b-back. Just, please..."

An old kitchen towel floats into the periphery of my vision and before I have time to react, Patrick covers my nose and mouth. I try holding my breath, knowing there's likely some chemical on the cloth, but I end up coughing and sucking in air. A sweet smell fills my nostrils, and I blink back tears.

The world blinks in and out of focus and then goes completely black.

Chapter 2

Alister

I clear away the last of the fallen branches, throwing them on top of the pile of debris from the storm last night. It's only a little past eight in the morning, but I've been up for hours. A lighthouse keeper's job is never finished.

Most lighthouses are purely aesthetic these days since ships have GPS, radar equipment, and other sophisticated nautical navigation tools. However, there are a few functioning lighthouses dotted along the coasts.

I've been on this rocky little island for six years now. Or is it seven? I don't bother marking the years down, since I don't want to remember what life was like before I came here.

My eyes slam shut, and I try to push away the darkness crawling out from the locked corners of my mind. The first few months here were hell. I came back from the military a broken shell of a man, inside and out. Damn left leg is scarred to hell, and hurts like a motherfucker when it rains, which is all the time.

I deserve the pain. I deserve to suffer for the way I failed my unit, and worse, my family.

My hands tighten into fists and I grit my teeth, tensing every muscle in my body as guilt crashes into me like a tidal wave. I hold my breath while drowning in dark regrets, only to surface again, gasping for air.

The breeze picks up, blowing through my wild hair and tangling the strands. I turn into the wind, facing the sea as I take a deep breath. The smell of salt, earth, and rain fills my lungs, and I'm grounded once more.

Opening my eyes, I survey the unrelenting water crashing against the rocks. Purple clouds gather in the distance, blocking out what little sunlight there is on this dismal, stormy morning. The muted color palette suits me just fine.

Continuing my walk around the perimeter, I force myself to focus on all the little repair projects that need to be done. Replacing some of the stones around the base of the lighthouse. A fresh coat of paint when we get a stretch of sunny days. The rickety stairs leading down to the shore needed replacing when I bought this island, but I haven't bothered yet. No one visits, and I sure as hell try not to leave except for supply runs.

I'm not lonely, though. I like my solitude. Besides, this old lighthouse keeps me busy. If it's not repairs and maintenance, it's logging the weather patterns and doing daily reports to the Coast Guard.

This island is only large enough to hold a lighthouse and a few storage sheds, so I don't get a lot of action. Still, when I bought this hunk of deserted land, I knew it was my responsibility to keep everything running. It's good. It gives me purpose, which is something I was severely lacking when I got out of the military.

I shake my head and rub my eyes, hoping to stop the ever-looming pit of darkness from swallowing me whole. Not today. I have too much shit to do.

The storm last night was only a teaser for what's to come in the next few days. According to the radar and weather reports, a more aggressive storm is headed this way. I still need to check on the sheds and make sure everything is tied down and locked up tight, then it's back up to the top to clean the windows and lenses in preparation for tonight.

Taking another healing breath of the salty sea air, I run through the list of things to do before the next storm hits in a few hours. I'm about to turn away from the gray skies and choppy waves when something catches my eye.

I walk out on the rocky ledge that hangs over the shore to get a closer look. At first, all I see is a soggy pile of what appears to be black clothes, or perhaps a blanket. Strange, but not concerning. I get random shit on this shore all the time, being so close to New York and Massachusetts.

But then it moves.

I'm frozen in place while the black blob sways from one side to another, then collapses. A gust of wind picks up some of the black cloth, pulling it back to reveal a face.

Every protective instinct I thought I'd lost comes rushing forward, choking me as I leap over the ledge and land on the pebbled shore with a thud. My left leg screams at me, but I ignore it, picking up my speed.

I fall to my knees in front of the woman, noting her deathly pale face and blue lips. Her eyes flutter, but then close, as if she's trying to wake up. She's wrapped in dark clothes, which are soaked. I check for a pulse, breathing a sigh of relief when I pick up a steady thrum against my fingers.

My field medic training kicks in, and I assess the woman for damage. Scanning the shoreline, I look for a boat that might have crashed or anyone else that could be with her. I don't see anything. I'm not sure why the tightness in my chest loosens. It can't be because I'm glad she's alone. That's just cruel. I don't care if she has someone with her. A man, or whatever. I don't know her.

Jesus, not the time, I scold myself.

Looking down at the woman in front of me, I notice the delicate curve of her lips, the slight upturn of her nose, and soft, round cheeks that make her look adorable and cuddly.

I mean, seriously, what the hell is wrong with me?

Carefully, I slip one arm under her shoulders, lifting her slightly before sliding my other arm under her knees. I stand with the woman in my arms, shocked when she stirs slightly and curls her body around mine. She buries her nose into the side of my neck and clutches my jacket like she's trying to burrow into me.

The absolute batshit crazy thing is... I want her to.

Nope. I'm no prince saving a damsel in distress. I'm more like an ogre trying to do the right thing and praying I don't scare the crap out of this sweet creature when she wakes up.

Eyeing the stairs I've neglected to fix, I curse myself and hike up the steep incline without their help. Looks like that project just got bumped to the top of the list. If I had functioning stairs, I could be at the lighthouse that much faster. For some reason, this woman's comfort and safety have become my new number one priority.

Running as fast as I can without risking falling and hurting my precious cargo, I finally make it to the lighthouse. I bound up the stairs, taking them two at a time while ignoring the lightning bolts of pain shooting up my left leg.

I make it to my loft and head straight to my bedroom, laying the woman on my bed. I check for a pulse again, nodding to myself when I feel it. Brushing her hair out of her face, I notice the woman has a cut on her forehead, right below her hairline. It's not deep, but head wounds bleed a lot.

I'm about to grab my first aid kit to clean her up when she shivers and heaves out a shuddering breath. Her teeth clatter, jarring me out of my daze. Shit. She's freezing in those wet rags.

I don't hesitate to strip her of her clothes. There's no time for propriety where hypothermia is concerned. I can't help but notice how tiny she is. This woman has curves, even though I know I shouldn't be looking, but she's so short, I feel like wrapping her up and sticking her in my pocket.

Where the fuck did that thought come from?

I grab a towel from the bathroom, quickly drying her inky black hair and cleaning up her wound before removing my clothes. I pull on a clean pair of boxers, but that's it. She needs my body heat. She doesn't need to see my cock getting hard for the first time since moving out here. Fucker must be confused.

I take a second to calm the hell down, giving my unruly dick a talking to. This is about saving the siren who washed up on my shore, not satisfying my base needs. I'm not a good man by any stretch of the imagination, but I'm not a monster.

I crawl under the blankets with my mystery woman, turning her so her back is facing me. I wrap an arm around her waist, pulling her closer to my chest. Fitting my legs up against hers, I press us as close together as possible.

She fits perfectly in my arms. Her head is tucked under my chin as her curves melt into the hard slats of my muscles. I know this woman doesn't belong to me, and that I'm only doing this to warm her up, but for one moment I let myself pretend she's mine.

After a few minutes, I feel the heat returning to her core. I rub my hand up and down her arm to encourage blood circulation. I stay curled around the little siren until I'm satisfied she's nice and toasty.

It takes far more effort than I'd like to admit to untangle myself from her. Digging through my dresser, I find a gray t-shirt and sweatpants. I know they'll be huge on her, but I don't want the woman to wake up naked and assume the worst.

After dressing her, I grab another blanket from the couch and tuck it around the woman, making sure she's safe and secure.

I stand over her for a few breaths, studying her beauty. Already, her cheeks are a peachy pink instead of ghostly white, and I'm unreasonably satisfied that I helped warm her up.

Remembering the cut on her forehead, I rush to the bathroom to grab my first aid kit. I gently sit next to the woman, tucking a few strands of hair behind her ear so I can get a better look at her wound.

I take my time applying ointment and a gauze pad, making a note to check on it in a few hours. She doesn't need stitches, but if the cut is still open, I might have to use some butterfly bandages.

My thumb traces over the outer edge of the gauze pad, meandering down her cheek before brushing across her soft, full lips.

Precious.

There's that word again. I've only ever thought it around this woman, and I'm not sure what that means. I should leave her be. Let her rest. It's not like she's going anywhere when she wakes up.

Even as I tell myself that, I grab a wooden chair from my small dining room table and place it right next to the bed before plopping down. There are a dozen projects I need to get done, but I can't seem to bring myself to move from my seat. In fact, I can't even look away from the enchanting sleeping beauty in my bed.

Who are you, little siren? And why did the sea bring you to me?

Chapter 3

Delaney

A rhythmic noise pulses around me as I slowly become aware of my body. I can't quite open my heavy eyelids yet, but I can feel cool air on my lips and cheeks, as well as a soft blanket cocooned around me.

The steady cadence of the sound comes into focus, and I realize it's waves lapping against the shore.

Waves. Water. Boat. Brothers...

My heart thrashes around in my chest and panic crawls up my throat, choking me as I jerk upright. A searing pain slices through my skull, causing my temples to throb. I force my eyes open, wincing against the light.

"It's okay," a deep, scratchy voice says from beside me.

I snap my head in that direction, swallowing down a sob as the world blurs and tilts. My stomach somersaults, and I'm worried I may be sick.

Blinking a few times, my vision slowly adjusts to my surroundings, though every muscle aches and every nerve ending seems to be firing at once. My heart jackhammers against my ribcage, making it hard to take a full breath.

Holy. Crap.

I stare at the man sitting next to me, noting his huge frame, despite being curled up in a chair. Dark brown eyes peek out from a mess of darker hair, and suddenly I'm breathless for a whole different reason. The muscles in his shoulders bunch up, and he dips his head down while holding his palms out, facing me.

Is he trying to make himself smaller? Less intimidating?

That thought softens me toward him, though I'm still sore, scared, and confused as hell.

"Who... who are you?" I stutter. The words get stuck in my throat, and a cough steals the air from my lungs. Every muscle strains and aches, and my head feels like it's going to burst from the pressure.

"Here," the man next to me says.

He hands me a glass of water, which I gladly take. I feel a hand on my back, rubbing gentle circles between my shoulder blades as I sip the refreshing liquid.

"That's it, little siren," he encourages, his voice barely above a whisper.

The heat from his hand and the gentle motion of his fingers stroking my back calms me down enough to take a breath. My muscles unclench, and I find myself leaning into his touch. I close my eyes, then snap them open when the room starts to spin.

The man wraps his fingers around the cup in my hand, taking it from me before I spill it. "Take it easy, now."

The gravelly tone resonates somewhere deep inside me. It's comforting in a way I'm not used to. When was the last time someone wanted me to take it easy? Never, if I had to guess. Why do I want to do whatever this man tells me? Damn, I must have hit my head when my brothers...

Fear seizes my lungs once again, and a tremor works its way down my spine. "Who are you?" I ask again, more forcefully this time.

"Alister."

"Why am I here?"

"I found you washed up on my shore. Figured you could use a place to rest and recuperate."

I risk a glance at him, wanting to see if he's for real. I've spent my life around shady characters and skilled liars, so I'd like to think I'm good at sniffing them out. Then again, I didn't notice my brothers were keeping tabs on me and wanted to sell me, so maybe I'm not that bright after all.

"Who else is here? How long have I been out? Did you tell anyone you found me?" The questions pour out, my voice getting higher and more shrill with each word. I'm gasping for air at the end, the stitch in my side protesting with each ragged breath. My eyes never leave his, even as I struggle to get myself under control.

Alister slowly reaches out, as if not wanting to startle me. He rests his huge palm right over the center of my chest, pressing down slightly. I'm about to jerk away from him, but the pressure feels... good. Grounding. Surprisingly, I can breathe easier, my chest rising and falling beneath his palm.

"That's good," he whispers, his words soothing me as much as his steady touch.

My heart beats against Alister's palm, slowing with each passing second. I no longer feel out of control, tossed around by fear and indecision. Peering into his eyes once more, I notice swirls of caramel and gold shining in the depths of his brown irises. I can't look away. Each inhale ties me closer to this man, each exhale strengthening whatever bond we're forming.

"To answer your questions, it's just me here in this lighthouse. I found you early this morning, and you've been sleeping for about eight hours. I don't have anyone to tell about your sudden appearance in my life, and even if I did, I haven't had time to say anything since I've been watching over you..." He trails off, clearing his throat and looking away from me.

Is he embarrassed? About what? Wait, did he just say he spent eight hours by my side?

My hand moves on its own, my palm flattening over Alister's heart. He closes his eyes and breathes in deep as I press my hand into the hard planes of his chest. Alister flexes, his muscles rippling under my touch.

When he opens his eyes, they are full of wonder and awe, like he can't believe I'm touching him.

Deep brown eyes lock onto mine, widening slightly when I stare right back. I take in Alister's furrowed brow, strong jaw, and slightly crooked nose. He's all sharp angles and cut muscles and somehow, I know he's as weary as I am. Exhausted from trying to survive the hand life dealt him. I can feel the weight of whatever he's been carrying, see it in the way he holds himself.

What secrets are you hiding, gentle giant?

Long, dark lashes frame his brown eyes, softening his look ever so much. The slight stubble on his chin makes him look as rugged and weathered as the rocky shores of this island. Alister opens his mouth, then closes it again, drawing my attention to his full lips.

I break eye contact and let my hand drop, heat rising in my cheeks. I shouldn't gawk at the man who saved me. As far as I can tell, he's just as surprised to see me as I am to see him, which is a plus in the truthful column. Alister hasn't harmed me, and I'm not tied up in any way. I could make a run for it if I wanted, but where would I go? I don't even know where I am, or who, if anyone, is after me.

Alister removes his hand from my chest, and I'm surprised when I feel empty and untethered. "Thank you," I whisper, tangling my fingers in the baggy gray shirt I'm wearing.

Wait. Baggy gray shirt? I don't own a baggy gray shirt.

I tug at the material, then lift the blanket covering my legs. I'm drowning in a pair of sweatpants that no doubt belong to the man sitting next to me.

Tilting my head, I give him a questioning look.

"I was afraid of you catching hypothermia from your soaking wet clothes," he answers immediately, already knowing the direction of my thoughts. "Washed 'em this morning after cleaning you up. They're hanging out to dry right now."

I nod, then wince at the sharp pain radiating through my head.

"You had a nasty cut on your forehead," Alister continues. "Patched you up, but I'll need to check it soon."

"Thank you," I say again, hating how weak my voice sounds. I'm suddenly drained of what little energy I had, and my eyes close on their own before I snap them open again. I have more questions that need answering.

"Anyone woulda done the same," he drawls.

"That's not true," I say before thinking better of it.

My own flesh and blood didn't save me. They were the ones who left me to die in the first place. More memories of the last twenty-four hours flood my mind.

Waking up in the trunk of a car. Being carried through the docks and tossed onto a boat.

Derek was there, but I don't remember seeing anyone else. He wouldn't look at me.

Inky waters lapping at the small boat. Angry clouds blocking out the moon and stars.

I remember my limbs felt impossibly heavy, and it took all of my energy just to tilt my head up and keep my eyes open. I somehow picked myself up and stumbled...

And fell into the icy water.

I shiver and close my eyes, going back to the moment my body plunged into the unforgiving waters. Coughing and sputtering, I waved my arms in some desperate attempt to get my brother to save me. Idiot.

I barely remember Derek's shocked face as he stared down at me, bobbing in the water. A moment of regret bled through his otherwise rough exterior, followed by grief. Then, he hardened his features and stared right at me.

"It's better this way. Swim if you can. Get away and don't come back."

I have no doubt he was supposed to kill me, and for all he and anyone else knows, I'm dead. I *should* be dead. I don't remember anything after watching the boat grow smaller and smaller.

"Hey, now," Alister whispers, his large hand wrapping around mine. His thumb brushes back and forth over my knuckles, that one simple touch making it easier to breathe. "I want to hear your story, little siren. But you need more rest. I don't know what you're runnin' from, but you're here now. You're safe."

I blink back tears, then flip my hand over, lacing my fingers through his. Alister grunts and I try to pull my hand away. *What was I thinking?* But then he squeezes my fingers, reassuring me he's right here.

How did this man become my anchor in a sea of chaos and confusion?

Alister gently guides me so I'm laying down again, adjusting my pillows until he's satisfied with my comfort level. I try to keep my eyes open, but they close on their own. A blanket tightens around me, and I know Alister is tucking me in. I swear I feel his lips brush across my forehead, but maybe I'm dreaming.

I'll just rest for a little bit, then I'll come up with a game plan. My brothers didn't want me to survive, but Alister had other plans. I'll have to thank him properly before going on my way, but I'm too tired right now.

Yes, a short nap, then I'll regroup.

As sleep pulls me under, I'm already doubting whether the muscled giant is real or a figment of my imagination. Maybe I died after all and ended up in ripped Greek god heaven. Another question that will need to be answered once I wake up.

Chapter 4

Alister

Sunlight streams through a window in my room, the bright yellow rays startling me from my sleep. *What time is it?* I can't remember the last time I woke up after sunrise.

Stretching, I groan as my back pops a few times. My left leg spasms, the pain ramping up my heart rate. Why am I so sore?

Waking up a little more, I notice I'm on the floor. Then it hits me. The mystery woman from yesterday.

I sit straight up, looking over at the bed. It's empty, and fear strikes at my core. The pain long forgotten, I scramble to stand, noticing for the first time that I'm tangled up in blankets. Cursing, I throw them off of me, then run a hand through my hair.

Where could she have gone? I need to check her bandages again and feed her. I didn't get a chance to give her any food yesterday before she passed out on me. Dammit, I should have insisted on a bowl of soup or something.

A soft, tinkling noise filters through my thoughts, drawing my attention away from the mounting worry lodged deep in my chest. I turn toward the sound, my feet carrying me out of my room and into the small kitchenette.

I freeze in my tracks at what I see.

A curvy little goddess is stirring something, her back facing me as she sways her round hips back and forth while humming to herself. She's only wearing the t-shirt I gave her yesterday, which falls just past her knees. She's so damn short and soft and adorable.

I get the insane urge to walk up behind her, slide my arms around her waist, and pull her against me. I want to bury my nose into the side of her neck and breathe her in, fuse her scent, her entire being with mine.

Stop it, I scold myself. I don't even know her name. I can't want forever with her. Plus, she's vulnerable right now. I don't know what the hell she escaped, or how she ended up on my shore, but she doesn't need a surly bastard lusting after her. I'd only hurt her in the long run. It's all I know how to do; cause pain and destruction.

Despite my stern pep-talk, my eyes wander down her figure, following the slight dip in her waist, the curve of her round hips, leading down to thick thighs I can't help but picture wrapped around my neck while I lick her to orgasm.

Jesus Christ. Totally inappropriate.

I notice her feet are bare, which doesn't sit right with me. I run back to the bedroom and grab a pair of wool socks. They'll go all the way up her calves, but at least she won't catch a chill. The floors in here are concrete, and I haven't gotten around to getting rugs or anything like that. Never even considered it. But now I wish I would have furnished the place more, made it look like someone is living here.

Then again, I haven't really been living. Surviving, maybe, though some days that's questionable. As I walk back into the kitchen, studying the silhouette of the little siren, something clicks. I feel a monumental shift, my chest tightening and then relaxing as I breathe in. She's a part of me. And I don't even know her goddamn name.

"Here." The word comes out as a harsh command, and I wince at my lack of social skills.

The woman turns to look at me over her shoulder, and I brace myself for her reaction. *Did I scare her? Does she want to leave? Will she…?*

And then she smiles.

It hits me like a tsunami, crashing into me and overwhelming every one of my senses. I don't know how I can feel her warmth and radiance from twenty feet away, but it's there all the same, washing over me and pulling me under.

"Hey," she says, her magical eyes twinkling. They aren't brown or green, but some swirling combination of both, along with flecks of blue and gold. Technically, I think they are hazel in color, but the kaleidoscope of shades and pigments is so much more than that.

"Socks," I stutter out like an idiot. I take a few steps toward her, holding out the socks in front of me like a pathetic offering.

The woman looks at my outstretched hand, then at me. Her smile turns into a grin, and holy hell, I'm lightheaded from all of my blood rushing south.

"Thank you, but I like going barefoot if you don't mind."

I stare at her, then look down at her feet, her little toes wiggling. "You'll get cold," I state, still holding out the socks. I don't know why I care so much. If she doesn't want to wear socks, that's fine.

Except, it's not. I have this unrelenting need to take care of her, protect her light, and vanquish anything or anyone that threatens her.

Before I even know what I'm doing, I kneel on the floor in front of her and carefully lift her right leg. She grasps onto my shoulders to keep her balance, but she lets me slip the wool sock on and pull it up her calf. I put the other sock on her left foot, grunting in satisfaction.

Looking up into the little siren's ethereal eyes, I see an array of emotions, ranging from disbelief to gratitude. Her pouty pink lips twitch, and soon she's grinning down at me. I try returning her smile, but it feels clunky and unnatural.

"You're kind of bossy," she says, though she's still grinning.

"What's your name?" I blurt out as I stand up.

We're close, much closer than I anticipated. She rests her palms on my chest, steadying herself. I wrap my hands around her hips, anchoring her to me.

She nibbles her bottom lip, her gaze dropping from mine. Interesting. She doesn't know if she can trust me with her name. This woman must be in more trouble than I originally thought.

Without thinking, I tip her chin up with my thumb, then cup the side of her cheek. I don't know what I'm doing or what to say, but I want to convince her she can tell me anything. She has no reason to trust me, but she has to feel this connection. Right? Am I going crazy? Maybe I've been cooped up in this lighthouse all alone for too long.

"Delaney," she whispers, finally gifting me with her gorgeous eyes. She looks so vulnerable, so fucking beautiful and pure, I can hardly take a breath.

"Delaney," I repeat in a whisper, feeling each syllable on my tongue.

I drop my hand from her face and take a step back. I don't want to crowd her or make her uncomfortable. I have no idea what the hell I'm doing or how this woman got under my skin without even exchanging more than a handful of words.

Delaney sways toward me, then catches herself, leaning back on the counter instead. Did she want me to keep holding her? No, that's just wishful thinking.

"Have you ever thought about planting some daffodils out front? Or wild roses? Oh! And tulips!"

I'm taken aback by her abrupt change of subject, but I try to form some sort of answer. "No." *Good one. That'll charm her.*

"Hmm," she responds, nodding thoughtfully. "They would add a nice pop of color."

I nod, unsure of how to follow up. God, I suck at personal interaction. There's a reason I'm out on this rock and not in regular society.

"I've always wondered," Delaney mercifully continues, "if lighthouses have to be painted with the red and white swirly stripes? Or can you do them in any color you want? Have you considered blue and yellow? Or maybe green and purple. But like a lime green. You know, to stand out for the boats to see."

My lips pull into an easy smile as I watch her chatter away. I think I'd like to have her here in my kitchen asking me about lighthouse color palettes every single morning for the rest of my life.

"Red and white are standard, but the rules are much more relaxed these days."

"Gotcha. Well, just something to consider, then."

She shifts her weight from foot to foot, her fingers playing with the hem of the large shirt she's wearing. Dammit, I'm being awkward, but I don't know how to fix it.

"What are you working on?" I finally ask, fixing my gaze on the bowl sitting on the counter.

"Pancakes!" Delaney answers cheerfully, seemingly happy with something else to talk about.

"I have stuff to make pancakes?"

She laughs, the sound flitting through the air and brightening the stuffy space. "It just takes the basics. Sugar, flour, salt. Usually, there are eggs involved, but I couldn't find any. I saw you had some applesauce in the pantry, however, which makes a great substitute. Plus, they'll have a slight cinnamon apple taste."

I stare at her thoughtfully. She might as well be speaking a foreign language.

Delaney must sense my confusion. She smiles again, then turns around and scoops up some of the batter, pouring it onto a preheated skillet I didn't notice before. "Just trust me. It'll be good."

"I do," I answer automatically.

She pauses, looking at me over her shoulder.

"You don't have to cook for me. You should be resting."

Delaney waves her hand in the air dismissively as she flips the partially cooked pancake. "I'm fine," she says.

I get the feeling she's always fine, even when her world is falling apart. "You almost drowned yesterday," I remind her, my voice harsher than I meant.

Her shoulders stiffen, then drop. I want to punch myself in the face. "But I didn't," she finally responds, shaking off whatever dark thought was passing through her mind. "And I have you to thank for that." Her voice is chipper again like she's used to bouncing back whenever life knocks her down. "So go sit at the table while I serve up!"

I'm about to protest, but then she levels a look at me, one eyebrow arching up, challenging me to defy her again. Fuck me, that look has my dick springing to life, and I reluctantly take a seat before she can see the effect she has on me.

A few minutes later, Delaney sets a plate stacked with pancakes down in front of me. She grabs a plate for herself, then brings over butter, applesauce, and two glasses of water. "I couldn't find syrup, but I firmly believe butter can make up for almost any missing ingredient."

I nod at her sage wisdom, and she gives me another smile.

We dig into our food, and I can't help the strangled moan that rumbles out of me at the first bite. It's been a long damn time since I've had pancakes and nothing as fluffy and delicious as these.

"Good?" Delaney asks.

I nod eagerly while shoveling another bite into my mouth. She stares at my lips, her cheeks turning the cutest shade of pink before she looks away.

"You like cooking?" I ask, making a concentrated effort not to inhale my breakfast like the brute I am.

"I..." Delaney tilts her head to the side, staring off into space. "I guess I've never really thought about it. No one has ever asked me what I like," she says more to herself than to me.

I want to ask a million different questions, but I bite my tongue, waiting for her to volunteer more information.

"I've always cooked, I guess. But I do enjoy it. Creating something from random ingredients, finding a good recipe, and then tweaking it to make it even better..." She trails off, lost in her thoughts. "Anyway, um... how about you?"

She's suddenly laser-focused on her food, cutting it up into smaller and smaller pieces. Her dark hair shifts forward as she dips her head, covering her face like a curtain. Damn, she's got her secrets, alright. I'll figure them out. I hope. I'm not the best conversationalist.

"It's been a while since I've cooked anything worthwhile. It's mostly fish, rice, and beans for me. Though I used to be able to whip up a mean lasagna. Fried chicken, too. My sister used to love my chicken cordon bleu."

I wince at the mention of my family. I don't want to talk about it. I don't want to remember. How did the little siren pull that information out of me without even trying?

"Sister? Does she live around here?"

"No," I snap. Delaney jumps at my tone, and I growl at myself for scaring her, which of course doesn't help the situation. "Sorry," I say more softly. "I... It's a long story."

Delaney catches my eyes, her light and goodness shining through. "I get it," she whispers, giving me a small smile. Christ, she's too good. Too pure.

We finish breakfast in silence, though it's not uncomfortable. Delaney stands and starts to clear the table, but I grab our plates before she can.

"Shower's in there," I say, pointing down the short hallway. "You can clean up and rest some more. I need to check on a few things outside and prepare for the next storm."

"Storm?"

I nod in confirmation. "Might be a few days until I can get you back home. No one is going to want to sail or fly out here until things have settled down."

"Home?" she squeaks.

I turn to look at her, noting how she curls in on herself. Once again, I find myself drawn to her, and I wrap my hand around hers, squeezing lightly. "Or wherever you want to go." I desperately want to know what put that fear in her eyes, and why she doesn't want to go home. Now isn't the time, though. "But for the next few days, we can be roommates." I nearly choke on the word. *Roommates?* More like soulmates.

Crazy bastard, my inner voice shouts.

Delaney breathes out, relaxing at my words. She doesn't have to go anywhere ever again. In fact, I think I'd be happy if I tucked her into my side and kept her next to me forever.

First, I need to figure out what she's running from. Then I'll make her mine.

Chapter 5

Delaney

I gaze across the gray, choppy waters, noting how far away the nearest shoreline is. Miles and miles, Alister told me. I'm thankful for each one. I know I'll have to come up with a more permanent life plan sooner or later, but staying here with Alister is starting to feel natural. Easy. Perfect.

Today marks day four of my tenure at the lighthouse. Another storm came and went yesterday and this morning, Alister got up early to check everything and clear up debris. I volunteered to help, and even though the stubborn giant insisted I needed to rest, I managed to get him to agree to an hour of outdoor time.

He's been keeping an eye on me the last half an hour as if he thinks I'm going to suddenly collapse. It's sweet, but I'm not sure how to handle this level of care and attention. I won't lie, it makes me feel all warm inside like I'm seen, understood, and cherished. It's a dangerous thing to want, and a scary thing to get used to. Will I ever find anyone else who looks at me the way Alister does?

The breeze picks up, and I snuggle deeper into the fleece-lined coat Alister gave me this morning. It's huge on me, and I love it. I'm surrounded by his spicy, sea salt scent, and it's taking quite a bit of effort not to huff it in like a weirdo.

I can't help it, though. Everything about the lumbering lighthouse keeper comforts me. Even his unpracticed smiles and grunted words. I don't think Alister has had company, let alone a roommate, in quite some time. I know for a fact he hasn't had fun or laughed in way too long. I want to give that to him, bring his light back.

"How's it looking over there?" Alister calls out, ripping me away from my thoughts.

"All clear!" I answer, taking one last look across the shoreline for any branches we missed while cleaning up.

Turning back toward the lighthouse, I see Alister standing tall, his arms crossed over his chest as he stares at me. The first few days I was with him, I thought he was annoyed or frustrated with me when he looked at me like that. But now, I have a sneaking suspicion it's a possessive look.

Or at least that's what I've been fantasizing about these last several nights. I've been able to keep my surprisingly dirty thoughts to myself during the day, but they've infiltrated my dreams. As soon as I close my eyes, I picture Alister joining me in bed, climbing over me, surrounding me with strength and certainty. He kisses me, soft and slow at first, and then something in him snaps. I dream about devastating, toe-curling, soul-shifting kisses from the reclusive Greek god of a man who sleeps on the floor next to me. And all this from the mind of someone who has little to no experience with the opposite sex.

It's confusing and exhilarating, but I'm sure my affections are misplaced. Alister is the first man to treat me with any level of respect, but that doesn't mean he's in love with me. He said it himself, he would have helped out anyone who washed up onshore.

Alister is a good person, though I don't think he sees himself that way. He's hiding something, just like me. The difference is, I don't think his secrets will endanger anyone's life.

"You cold?" Alister asks when I'm a few feet away from him. Before I even answer, he's taking his hat off and putting it on my head, rolling up the edge so it doesn't cover my eyes.

I smile at his thoughtfulness, delighted when his lip twitches and his chocolate brown eyes light up with a caramel swirl.

"How do I look?" I ask, turning my head from side to side.

When my gaze lands back on Alister, I can't quite read the look on his face. My cheeks heat, despite the cool wind and damp air. *Why did I say that? What was I expecting him to say?*

"Stunning," Alister murmurs.

I blink a few times, not sure I heard him correctly. He tips his head back and runs a hand through his hair as if he's feeling awkward or embarrassed. Around me? It's kind of... adorable.

"Thanks," I say with a smile. "It's the latest nautical fashion trend. I think it pairs perfectly with the oversized jacket and boats for shoes," I tease, lifting a foot to show him what I mean. Alister lent me an old pair of boots, which of course were ten sizes too big.

"Is that so?" Alister asks, amusement lacing his words. He lifts a dark eyebrow at me, giving me an almost playful look.

Good god, he's too sexy when he does that. I'll be seeing that little grin in my dreams tonight. "Mmhm," I nod, twirling to add the right effect.

My feet slip in my shoes, and I stumble off-balance, jerking forward to keep from falling off the edge of the overhang. Alister grabs my hand and pulls me toward him, spinning me and dipping me as if we're ballroom dancers.

I peer into those deep brown eyes, breathing in everything about him, about this moment. Alister spreads one hand out over my lower back, his other hand supporting me between my shoulder blades.

"Good catch," I whisper, giving him a soft smile.

Alister doesn't waiver, doesn't even blink as his eyes lock onto mine. He's digging around in my chest, opening up my heart, and settling deep down in my soul. There's no other way to describe it.

The air stills around us, and I'm not sure if it's our connection or the weather, but the atmosphere shifts, turning purple and fuzzy at the edges. I can't look away. This man is baring himself to me in a single look. I don't need his words when I can *feel* the intensity of his emotions.

Alister is impenetrable to everyone except me. His brow furrows, and I know he feels it, too. Confusion eventually turns to acceptance. He holds me, suspended in his grip as the last of his defenses fade away.

Somewhere in the distance, a brilliant light flashes in the sky, followed by rolling thunder threatening to tear the heavens in two. But none of that matters at this moment.

Alister's breath tickles my skin, his nose brushing against mine. He pauses, searching my eyes for any sign of discomfort. I wrap my arms around his neck, pulling the beautifully rugged man closer. Our lips touch as the sky cracks open, drenching us in seconds.

Alister doesn't stop. He angles his head, slanting his mouth over mine as he goes for a deeper kiss. I open up for him, tasting sweet rainwater on his tongue. Alister groans, tightening his hold on me as he fuses our lips together.

He slides his tongue against mine, then tickles the roof of my mouth, making me whimper. My sexy lighthouse keeper grunts in satisfaction, standing upright as he hauls me up into his arms. I automatically wrap my legs around his torso, panting for air. Alister grips my thighs, sliding his palms up to my ass, where he holds me and massages my flesh.

I rest my forehead on his, cold rain pelting me and dripping down my hair into his face. Alister doesn't mind. He nuzzles into me, then tips my head up, sipping from my lips once more. I'm vaguely aware of being carried inside.

We only make it up a few stairs before Alister presses my back against the wall and grinds his hard body against mine. I writhe beneath his commanding touch and desperate kisses. I feel his hands everywhere, sliding up my thighs, squeezing my breasts, threading his fingers through my hair and angling me just right.

I'm still catching my breath as he peels me off the wall and resumes his journey upstairs. We burst through the bathroom door, a tangled mess of soggy clothes and limbs. Alister sets me down on my feet, then immediately rips my coat off. I'm expecting him to do away with the rest of my clothes, but he stops, cupping my face in his hands.

"Is this okay?" he whispers.

I nod eagerly, smiling so he knows I'm totally on board with him doing whatever he wants. I might not know what that means, considering my lack of experience, but after that kiss? Yeah, I'm definitely going to need more.

"Talk to me, little siren. I've been fucking dying for a kiss, but I don't want to take advantage of you."

"I've been dying for a kiss as well," I tell him, not wanting to give away that it was my first. Alister nods but doesn't say anything. *How does he always seem to know there's more to my story?* "I... I'm good with, um... whatever you want to do," I say awkwardly.

Alister nuzzles into the side of my neck, peppering kisses and little nips along my throat until he reaches my ear. "And what do you think I want to do?"

His sexy tone travels through me, landing between my thighs. A dull, throbbing ache blooms there, and I know only Alister can take it away. "Shower together?" I squeak.

"Mmhm," he grunts, sucking on a sensitive spot between my neck and shoulder. "Among other things."

"Um... t-touch me?"

"Is that a question or a command, sweetheart?"

Oh, my god, why is that so hot? Liquid pleasure spikes my veins, weaving in and out of my muscles and making me pulse with anticipation.

"Will you touch me?" I whisper, biting my bottom lip.

Alister's eyes turn black, and his fingers curl around the hem of my shirt. Slowly, he lifts it, and I raise my arms, helping him to take it all the way off. A strangled groan rumbles up from his chest, and then he brushes the back of his knuckles over my breasts, tickling my sensitive nipples.

I shudder and tip my head back, moaning when he palms my breasts and squeezes them in his large hands.

"Fucking perfect," he growls.

Alister continues stripping me out of my clothes, then yanks off the huge shoes I'm wearing. I grab his shirt to peel it off, but Alister beats me to it. In record time, he's standing before me, completely naked.

My eyes wander down the cut muscles of his chest, his defined abs, and the chiseled V lines leading to...

"Holy shit," I blurt.

His thick shaft is ruddy, swollen, and freaking huge. A pearl of precum dribbles down from the slit on top, and I suddenly want to lick it up.

"Can't look at me like that, siren," he grits out. His hand wraps around his massive length, giving it a few pumps. "Gonna come before I even touch you."

My cheeks burn red, but his confession gives me confidence. This man sincerely finds me and my curves so irresistible, he's afraid he might fall apart before we even start.

He leans over, turning on the water and adjusting it to the right temperature. Alister takes my hand and gently pulls me closer. His hands glide up and down my sides, mapping out my curves. I stand on my tiptoes, pressing my mouth against his.

The kiss is like wildfire, spreading through my chest, lungs, core, and limbs. I'm burning up for more, more, *more.*

Alister backs me against the shower wall, leaning closer, so all I can see are his broad shoulders and dark brown eyes. I'm drowning in his scent, his heat, the intensity of his stare. Hot water splashes my skin, making me aware of every touch, every sensation rocketing through me.

"Can I taste you, little siren?" he murmurs, his voice coming from deep within his chest.

"T-taste me?" I whisper, looking up into those mesmerizing eyes. Dark brown mixes with lighter shades of caramel, and I even see a golden sparkle that hasn't been there before.

One massive hand trails down my body, cupping my breast before sliding down and squeezing my hip. I rock closer to him, my body crying out for more, even if I don't know what that means. Alister traces the outside of my pussy with his fingertips, teasing me and making me jolt.

He chuckles darkly as he continues stroking my throbbing sex. "Is all this for me?" he growls, dipping his head down to suck on my neck.

I let out a breathy moan as one finger slips into my folds, gathering up my arousal and rubbing gentle circles over my clit. "Yes," I choke, my knees wobbling at the sudden wave of pleasure spiking through my bloodstream. My nerves are firing all at once, every touch, every ragged breath coursing through me and drawing me closer to Alister.

My broody, sexy giant kneels in front of me, and my heart pounds out a staccato rhythm that vibrates throughout my body. An intense pressure blooms in my core, pulsing and growing with every beat of my heart. Alister stares at me for a long moment before twisting his lips up in a wicked grin.

I gasp when he dips his tongue into my slit, licking me from bottom to top. We both groan, seemingly lost in the intensity of the moment. He grabs my left thigh, spreading me open and guiding my leg over his shoulder. I grip his hair for support, inadvertently shoving him further into my aching core. He doesn't seem to mind.

Alister growls and squeezes my ass, flattening his tongue and tasting every inch of me, just like he said he wanted to. I feel him every-fucking-where. His lips wrap around my clit and he sucks lightly, making me convulse in his arms. Liquid heat pools in my pussy and drips into his mouth, making him growl in approval.

The pressure in my core expands, pressing on my nerve endings and making my skin prickle with awareness. My cunt pulses for him as he devours my swollen, sensitive flesh with his lips, teeth, and tongue.

Tension wraps around my muscles, pulling them tight against my skin. I feel my orgasm crawl up my spine, excruciatingly slow as Alister coaxes my pleasure from me, one lick at a time. He growls and bites down on my clit, the sharp sting sending me over the edge as bliss erupts from my core.

"Oh, f-f-fuck…" I cry out, my voice broken and breathy. I claw at his back, his shoulders, his head, anywhere I can find purchase.

He never lets up, never stops, never gives me a chance to catch my breath. Alister rolls his tongue against my clit once, twice, three times, and just as I'm about to succumb to another orgasm, he's gone. I whimper at the loss, but then shout out my pleasure when he thrusts a finger deep inside me and curls it up.

My back bows off the wall as a scream is ripped from my lungs. A violent orgasm tears through me, shredding up my insides as it claws its way out. I come in waves, each one more blissfully painful than the last.

When every ounce of pleasure is wrung from my bones, I deflate against the wall, sliding down into Alister's open arms.

"Holy wow," I breathe, curling up into his chest.

Alister grunts and holds me close. He's breathing just as heavily as I am. He's shaking a bit, too. "You come like a fucking goddess, do you know that? So damn beautiful."

We stay like that for long moments, Alister whispering soothing, sweet things into the shell of my ear while he holds me. Hot water beats down on us and steam curls around our tangled bodies.

Eventually, Alister stands, helping me up as well. He grabs the bar of soap from the shelf in the shower and begins washing every inch of me, massaging my sore muscles and calming me down with each steady stroke. I feel so precious, so utterly loved, a lump forms in my throat.

"Thank you," I whisper, my voice cracking at the end.

Alister turns me so I'm facing him, his hands lightly wrapping around either side of my neck. I tilt my head up, amazed by the concern and kindness I see in his eyes.

He doesn't say anything, he simply presses his lips to my forehead, as if kissing away all of my sadness. Surprisingly, it's very effective.

After a few moments, Alister shuts the water off and engulfs me in a big, fluffy towel. I giggle as he dries me off, messing with my hair and

"So, is your girl still with you?"

I don't bother correcting him about *my girl* this time. Last time we talked, I wasn't ready to admit how important the little siren had become to me in such a short period of time. Now? Well, now I know my life's purpose is to protect and support my sweet Delaney.

"Yeah," I respond, taking a few steps toward the balcony of the lighthouse. "She's... incredible," I admit.

"Congrats, man. I mean it. Did you find out what happened to her?"

"Ah, no, not exactly. I'm still working on it. She's been... distracting."

Theo chuckles. "I know what that's like. What's your plan?"

"Plan?"

"To keep her? Or... I didn't take you for a one-night stand kind of guy–"

"I'm *not*," I growl, wanting to set the record straight.

"Right, right," he mumbles. "Exactly. Have you talked to her about dating?"

"Dating?" I know I'm just repeating him like an idiotic parrot, but I'm sincerely lost here. "Not many venues on my island to take a beautiful woman on a date."

"Then is she moving in right away? I mean, she's already been staying with you."

"That's a little fast, don't you think?" Truthfully, I'd love for Delaney to stay with me forever, but it's too soon to make statements like that. I don't even know what life she left behind, let alone how to plan for a future.

"Nah," Theo answers easily. "When you know, you know. Like with my Emmaline. No matter the stakes, I wanted to be with her. Needed it."

"Yeah," I grunt in agreement. I get it. I need my woman, too, but I don't want to scare her away. "First, I need to figure out what she's running from. Then I'll convince her to stay with me. Or we can move. Maybe she wants to go out West, or hell, to another country," I muse, more to myself than to Theo.

"That's the spirit," he says with a chuckle. "Keep me posted. Maybe you should give Emmitt a call," he suggests, mentioning one of our buddies from the military. "I hear he's on leave and is checking out his old family ranch. He's got a lot of land and is looking for some help."

"I'm no rancher."

"It's hard work, but I know you'd be up for it. Just a thought, if you two want to start over somewhere new."

I hum and nod, considering his words. I like the idea of building a new life with Delaney.

We say our goodbyes, and I promise to call when I can. It's been years since I've chatted with anyone, let alone old military friends. Usually, it just brings back memories of my last deployment, and more specifically, what I came home to when all was said and done.

Checking my watch, I see it's just past noon. Delaney insisted on cleaning the kitchen this morning and said she'd have lunch ready for me by twelve-thirty. She's such a thoughtful partner, the kind I always envisioned myself with. That is, when I allowed myself to have such dreams.

I head down to the loft on the lower level of the lighthouse, stopping by the restroom to clean up for lunch. When I step into the kitchen, I'm greeted with the most perfect sight. Delaney is in another of my shirts, her hair piled on top of her head in a messy bun. Muted light comes in from the window, casting soft shadows over her delicate features.

And then the siren smiles at me.

Just like every time, her warmth radiates through me, drawing me closer until my arms are around her waist. I pull the curvy goddess against my body, leaning down to capture her lips.

She melts into my embrace, opening up for me and surrendering so sweetly.

We're both breathless by the time I pull away. I give her one last kiss on the forehead, loving the way it relaxes her. I don't think my girl has had a lot of love in her life. I'm not sure what I'm doing, but I want to give her everything she's been missing.

"Hello to you, too," Delaney says, beaming up at me before spinning out of my grasp. "Nothing too exciting for lunch today," she continues. "Just some soup and biscuits. I found an old box of Jiffy biscuit mix. It didn't have an expiration date, which is a little suspish to me. I tested one though, and I think we'll survive."

Her nose scrunches up adorably when she says *suspish*, and I struggle not to scoop her up and kiss that look off her face.

"Looks amazing," I tell her as we sit down.

She smiles at me, then digs in. This is my opportunity to talk to her like Theo said I should. If I can get her talking about one aspect of her life, maybe she'll open up about why she was half-drowned on my shore a few days ago.

"Do you work?" I blurt out. *Very smooth.*

Delaney tilts her head to the side, studying me. She nods her head slowly, then pauses before shaking her head no.

Glad she cleared that up.

"I used to work the night shift at a diner back in New York City."

"Did you quit? Get fired?" Is that an appropriate follow-up question? I suck at this.

"Well, after a week of no-shows, I'm guessing I'm not exactly employee of the month" she hedges. "Plus, it's not like I can go back to this city anyway," she mumbles.

I'm not sure if she meant for me to hear it or not. I'm about to demand she tell me more, but Delaney stuffs a biscuit in her mouth to avoid answering any more questions.

I sip at my soup, waiting for her to finish. This conversation needs to happen one way or another.

"How long have you lived in New York?" I ask.

"My whole life." Her eyes go wide at her admission. She seems to think she gave away some big mystery, but it's nothing. I want so much more.

"Any family waiting for you? Anyone we should call?"

"No."

That's all she says, but her tone is final. Okay... no talking about family. I try a different tactic.

"You said you enjoyed cooking, and I know you appreciate flowers. What else are you interested in?"

Delaney sets her spoon down and stares at me. I watch her defenses rise, protecting whatever secret she's holding so dear. "What's with the interrogation?"

"Just want to get to know the woman I had naked in my shower yesterday," I grunt.

I grab the last biscuit off my plate and pop it in my mouth, chewing with more force than necessary. I knew she was going to be hard to crack, but she's not giving me anything to work with.

I need to get some air and regroup. Come up with a better plan, better questions. I stand up, sliding my chair back from the table with a horrid screech. Delaney gasps, and I snap my eyes up, my heart lurching in my chest with what I see.

Delaney is curled in on herself, her arms wrapped around her torso as if she needs to protect herself from me. Her face is completely drained of color, and tears threaten to spill down her porcelain cheeks.

I close the distance between us, kneeling in front of her chair and grasping her hands in mine. "I'm sorry," I choke out. "Please don't ever be afraid of me. I would never hurt you. I couldn't. It's not possible."

Delaney blinks a few times, her eyes turning from dark green to light brown. Everything about her is magical and bright. All I want to do is protect that light.

"I don't know what I'm doing," I admit, dipping my head down to study our entwined fingers. "How can I keep you safe if I don't know what you're running from?"

I turn her hand over, tracing the lines of her palm before placing a kiss on the inside of her wrist. I guide her hand to rest on my chest, right over my heart. Just like that first morning when she woke up, I reach out and place my hand over her heart as well, reminding her of our connection.

"You can trust me," I murmur, leaning forward to kiss her forehead.

Delaney takes a deep breath, then surprises me by sliding off her chair and curling up into my lap. I hold her for long moments, tucking her head underneath my chin as I rub gentle circles on her back.

Jesus, I can feel her trembling, feel the pain and fear of whatever she's keeping locked up.

"Let it out, sweetheart," I whisper onto the top of her head, breathing in her sunshine and citrus scent. "I'm not going anywhere."

Finally, fucking *finally*, Delaney takes a cleansing breath, letting go of all the tension in her muscles.

"I was mostly raised by my older brothers, after my father..." she trails off, her voice so soft I have to strain to hear it. Still, at least she's talking. "After my father was killed for defaulting on loans from the Romano family."

"Fuck. I'm so sorry." I may be a recluse stranded on a little rocky island off the east coast, but I know who the Romanos are. One of the five organized crime families that run New York.

Delany shrugs, and my heart breaks for her even more. "It is what it is. My dad... I don't think he ever loved me. He always reminded me that I took his wife away, took my brother's mother away. She died during childbirth. I know it's not my fault, but at the same time, I understand his bitterness."

"What? No, Delaney. That's absurd. Grief or no grief, your father should never have made you feel that way. God, I'm so sorry you had to put up with that."

My sweet girl blushes and wipes away a few stray tears. "It's over now," she whispers. "Anyway, my brothers, Tim, Patrick, and Derek, mostly kept me around to cook and clean. They–"

"You don't ever have to cook again. Or clean. I'll do both," I immediately supply. What the hell were her brothers thinking? Delaney is too precious to be waiting hand and foot on three ungrateful bastards.

Delany giggles, the sound drawing me out of my dark thoughts. She cups my cheeks, the sparkle in her gorgeous eyes soothing my raw heart. "I like cooking for you," she says. "And I enjoy keeping our loft neat and tidy." She nibbles her bottom lip nervously before adding, "Not that it's *our* loft. It's yours, obviously. I'm just your roommate."

"You aren't *just* anything," I tell her, brushing my nose against hers. "And I think we've moved beyond roommate status, don't you?" I lift an eyebrow and give her my best grin.

Her eyes light up, her smile so big it must be hurting her cheeks. "What would you say we are?" she asks, her thighs tightening slightly around my torso. I don't even think she's aware of the subtle tilt in her hips, or the way she's rocking gently against me.

"We're real," I murmur into the side of her neck, trailing kisses up to the shell of her ear. "We're safe. We're forever, Delaney. You feel it too, right?"

She inhales sharply, tensing up in my arms. *Shit, was that too much, too soon?* But then my beautiful siren nods her head, slanting her lips over mine and owning me, body and soul.

I return her kiss with as much passion as she's giving me, my hands slipping beneath her shirt and caressing her soft skin. Delaney whimpers at my touch, her fingers diving into my hair and tugging with each stroke of her tongue.

I only have part of her story, but it's a start. I know my girl has been hurt, lied to, and manipulated by her family. I know her father had shady ties to the mafia. She didn't tell me her brothers were involved as well, but it wouldn't surprise me if they were. It's a hard life to escape from.

"Thank you for telling me more about you," I whisper, kissing her cheeks and nose. "I want your whole story, sweetheart. Every detail. But I know today was a lot." Delaney nods her head, relieved that I'm done grilling her. For now. "Can I reward you for being a good girl?"

Damn, just like that, my little siren's eyes shine with lust. She nods her head eagerly, wiggling on my lap.

I groan and stand up with my girl still in my arms. I love holding her, carrying her, having any part of her pressed against me. Fuck it, I just love *her*, period. I'm about to prove my unending devotion to the curvy goddess with my tongue, my fingers, and hopefully, my aching cock.

Chapter 7

Alister tosses me down on the bed, making me giggle. He falls on top of me, looking like a ravenous beast. I can't wait for him to devour me.

I curl my arms around his neck, pulling him down for a kiss. Alister opens for me and threads his fingers in my hair, angling me just right. The kiss goes from sweet to desperate, and he flips our positions so I'm on top. I lift myself, straddling him. I love the way his eyes darken as they roam up and down my body. He automatically runs his hands up my bare thighs and rests them on my hips, drawing me closer as he sits up.

I start rocking my hips against his thickening cock, leaning down to capture his lips once more. He growls, and I swear I can feel it down in my bones. I trail my hands down his chest, feeling every chiseled muscle until I get to the waistband of his sweatpants. I tug at the drawstring, but then I feel his hands covering mine.

"Delaney..."

"I want this," I whisper, looking him in the eye. "I want you to be my first."

Alister groans, then leans forward, resting his forehead on mine. "Fuck, little siren." He moves his hands back to my thighs as I start rocking against him again. Trailing his hands up toward my hips, he runs his mouth down my jaw, neck, and shoulder, nipping, licking, and kissing as he goes. "First and fucking last," he grunts.

Alister ravishes my mouth again with renewed energy and focus. I moan into his kiss as he slips his hands under the back of my shirt. He gently rolls us over so I'm on my back. Then he gets up off the bed and undoes the drawstring on his pants. I prop myself up on my elbows to enjoy the show. He pulls his pants and boxers down and stands at the foot of the bed completely naked, his cock standing at full attention, pointing right at me.

"Alister...holy crap, you're huge." I blush. I'm sure I sound so stupid and inexperienced. I mean, I've seen him naked before when we were in the shower, but I was a bit *distracted*, what with all the orgasms he gave me.

My man grins, and god, he's gorgeous when he does. I know he lost his smile a long time ago, and my heart grows three sizes knowing I had something to do with helping him find it.

"Thanks, baby. It's all for you." He kneels at the foot of the bed and grabs my ankles to pull me forward. "I can't wait to get inside of you, but I need you dripping for me."

He starts peeling my panties down my legs, tossing them behind him. Starting with my left foot, he blazes a trail of kisses, over my ankle, my calf, taking extra time to nip and lick at a sensitive spot behind my knee I didn't even know I had. Then he moves up to my inner thighs and I let out a needy sigh.

Placing my feet on the edge of the bed, Alister kisses up one thigh and then down the other, refusing to go to the one place I need him most.

"Alister... Please," I beg as I wiggle beneath him.

"I know, my sexy little siren. I'm taking my time with you. I promise I'll always take care of you." His hands move up my thighs and spread me wide open for him. I feel his hot breath a few inches away from my needy pussy. "You're so wet for me," he growls.

Lifting one leg over his shoulder, and then the other, he slides his hands under my ass and pulls me up towards his face. He circles his nose around the outside of my lips once, twice, three times. And then the teasing stops.

Alister flattens his tongue and licks me from bottom to top, making me cry out. He repeats the long, slow licks up my center. Each time his tongue hits my hard, swollen nub, I buck my hips. He brings his thumb to my clit and starts rubbing it in fast circles while his tongue thrusts in and out of my hole.

"Oh, my god... yes!"

He replaces his tongue with his finger, and I cry out again.

"You like that, baby? You like when I fuck your sweet pussy with my tongue and fingers?"

"Mmhm..." I breathe out, unable to put words together in a sentence.

Alister goes back to swirling his tongue over my clit, alternating between fast, slow, hard, and soft licks. It's driving me crazy. My legs start shaking and I move my hips toward him, running my fingers through his hair.

"That's it, baby. Ride my face. I fucking love tasting you."

He shoves two fingers into my entrance and curls them up, hitting some place deep inside that sends pleasure to every cell of my body. I'm right on the edge and he knows it. Sucking my clit into his mouth, Alister pumps his fingers faster and faster, giving me what I need.

"Alister... Alister... I'm..." I can't finish the thought. He's taking me higher and higher, and I know I'm about to snap.

"Come for me, Delaney," he commands.

Every muscle tenses, but I hold on to the sweet torture as long as I can. Alister gives me one last lick and I fly apart, free-falling into an ocean of sensation as wave after wave of ecstasy crashes over my body.

I feel his tongue move back down to my entrance as he laps up my juices, while his thumb presses against my clit, prolonging my orgasm.

I finally come down, my breaths ragged, my heart racing.

"Fuck. You're delicious."

I watch my beastly lighthouse keeper stand, never breaking eye contact as he crawls over me, placing his arms on either side of my head.

"Are you sure about this, baby girl?"

I nod my head and loop my hands around his neck, running my hands up the back of his head to pull him towards me.

Alister leans down and kisses me. It's wild and passionate, stealing the breath from my lungs. He breaks the kiss and ghosts his lips down my neck and across my collar bone. He reaches up and pulls the top of my shirt down until my right breast pops out. Alister rubs my pebbled nipple with his nose and then licks it before sucking my breast into his mouth.

"More," I moan.

He leans back and I whimper at the loss of his mouth.

"Relax, little siren. I've got you. I need you to take your top off."

"Oh." I blush.

"So eager." He grins as I pull my shirt over my head and lay back down.

His eyes roam over my breasts, down my belly, landing on my glistening pussy. He slowly drags his gaze back up over my body. I've never felt more wanted in my life.

"Delaney... so gorgeous."

Alister reaches out and runs his hands down my shoulders and over my breasts, where he takes time to rub both of my nipples. His fingers trail down my ribs, over my belly, and grip my hips. It's like he's memorizing every inch of my body with his touch. He leans down and places a tender kiss on my forehead, right over the bandage still covering my wound there.

"I'll be careful," he promises, the look in his eyes nearly making me tear up.

He brings his hands back to either side of my head and leans in for another breathtaking kiss before dropping his head to my breasts. Alister trails his nose and lips up and down the valley between my breasts and breathes me in. He takes my right nipple in his mouth, swirling and sucking. Then I feel a sting as he bites down, shooting lightning down to my clit.

"Yes! Alister!"

He grunts and sucks more of my breast into his mouth while kneading the other one in his hand. Finally, he pulls back with a pop before moving over to the other one and giving it the same treatment.

This time, when he bites down on one nipple, he pinches the other between his fingers. I feel it everywhere.

"Again," I moan.

He licks and kneads and then bites and pinches my nipples.

"Yes!" I feel myself soaking the sheets, gushing each time he bites down.

"Fuck, baby, I love your tits. I love how sensitive you are."

Alister continues to tease my nipples with his tongue and teeth and I start shaking.

"A-Alister, I think…"

He reaches down and presses his thumb down on my clit and I come. *Hard.*

"Goddamn," he grunts. "So hot. Love your sexy body. Jesus, you're incredible."

I'm still coming down from the unexpected explosion when I feel Alister drag his cock up and down my slit. Each time he hits my nub I shudder as tremors of my orgasm ripple out from my core.

"Are you sure you're ready for me, Delaney?"

"I'm sure. I want you."

He bends down and kisses me, sliding himself just a few inches inside.

"It's going to hurt a little. But I promise I'll be gentle. I'll make it so good for you. Do you trust me?"

"Yes," I say without hesitation.

He thrusts the rest of the way in. I feel a pinch as he tears through my virginity, stretching me wide.

Alister swallows my cry in a soul-crushing kiss. "I'm sorry, baby. Just relax. Breathe for me."

He kisses me again and stays still, letting me adjust to the new sensation of him inside of me.

"Are you okay?" His eyes are full of concern.

"Yeah, I feel so full. But good. I want more. Please, Alister."

He pulls out and I miss him, my pussy pulsing and feeling empty. Then he slowly strokes his cock inside of me again in a steady rhythm. It's gentle at first. He rolls his hips in shallow thrusts.

"More, Alister. I can take it. I want all of you."

Alister groans and drops his head to my chest, sucking on one nipple and then the other. His thrusts become deeper. I feel his balls slapping my ass and I moan. Each time he pushes his length inside, he brushes my clit, and I feel the coil start to wind in my belly.

"You feel so good. So hot and tight. I love being inside of you."

I moan and start to move with him.

"Fuck, baby. So good."

"Faster, please."

Alister leans back on his heels, angling my hips up, the new position hitting that spot deep inside of me that drives me crazy. He continues pumping in and out of me, pushing and pulling my body into him, fucking himself with my body.

Alister looks down between us and groans.

"Shit, Delaney. I love watching my cock disappear inside of you."

I tense up, feeling the orgasm start to take over. Two more thrusts and the coil inside me snaps.

"Alister! God, Alister," I moan over and over again, clawing at the sheets and throwing my head back.

He rubs my clit with his thumb, and I keep pulsing around his thick cock, pleasure prickling my skin as sweat drips down my forehead, between my breasts, and down my back.

"That's it. Fuck, milk my cock, beautiful." He thrusts once, twice, three times, and then stills. "I'm coming. Jesus, I'm coming so fucking hard."

Alister shakes as his orgasm overtakes him. I love seeing him lose control, love watching the pleasure cover his face as he lets go and finds his release. He shifts and comes down on top of me, holding himself up by his elbows, still buried deep inside my pussy.

He licks the sweat from between my breasts before sealing his lips over mine, sliding his tongue inside of my mouth, and drinking me in. We both groan as he pulls out of me. Alister pulls me close to him, tucking me into his side.

I drape a leg in between his and place my hand on his abs. He plays with my hair and kisses my forehead.

"Are you okay, siren?"

"Mmmhmm. More than okay." I smile up at him. He searches my eyes to make sure I'm telling the truth. "Is it always that good?"

He grins. "Only with you. Only you. You're perfect."

We stay tangled up in each other for a while before he gets up and heads to the bathroom. He comes back out with a washcloth, and I give him a questioning look. He smiles softly and proceeds to gently clean me between my legs. It's intimate in a different kind of way, but I feel so safe, so precious when he's taking care of me like this.

Alister cleans me up but doesn't dress me or put any clothes on himself either. Walking over to the other side of the bed, Alister pulls the covers over us and snuggles up close to me.

"Now get some sleep, precious. I'll be here when you wake up."

Chapter 8

Alister

Waking up next to Delaney has to be the best feeling in the world. Okay, sinking inside her snug little pussy was amazing too, and coming together... fuck, I'm hard already just remembering the way she trembled beneath me as her orgasm overtook her.

I look over at my sweet girl, taking in her dark eyelashes as they flutter against the soft, creamy skin of her round cheeks. Her black hair is a wild mess spread out behind her, and her pink, pouty lips curve up slightly, even in her sleep. In other words, she's radiant. Beauty personified.

I kiss her forehead, wanting to somehow communicate how precious she is, how she's changed everything about me without even trying. Then, I carefully roll Delaney onto her side and curl my large body around her smaller one.

The goddess in my arms stirs slightly, brushing her mouthwatering ass up against my morning wood. I swallow thickly, gritting my teeth against the need to plow into her right here, right fucking now. But my poor girl has to be sore this morning.

And yet, Delaney grinds down on me again, letting out a quiet little moan. I can tell she's still mostly asleep, but the fact that she still wants me in her foggy morning haze has my dick swelling even more, begging to get inside her wet, warm heaven.

I slide my hand over her curves, following the dip of her waist and the swell of her hip, where I hold her tightly and help her rub against me. I can tell the moment she fully wakes up. Delaney's soft gasp and full-body shiver cause me to buck my hips and slide my cock up and down the slit in her perfectly round ass cheeks.

"Alister..." she rasps out, her voice scratchy and sexy as fuck.

I have no doubt her throat is sore from screaming my name over and over yesterday. My chest swells up with pride at the memory of my sweet, filthy little Delaney creaming all over my cock. I did that to her. I made her sob with pleasure until she damn near passed out on me.

Delaney pushes her ass against my raging dick eagerly, letting the head of my cock tease her little entrance. I growl when I feel how wet she is, her sweet, sticky honey practically dripping out of her.

"You need something from me, baby?" I grit out.

"You know I do," Delaney practically whines. I'd chuckle, but I'm needier than her at this point and I feel her pain.

"I don't want to hurt you. We should probably take it easy today." I force the words out of my mouth even though I don't make any attempt to move out of our current position.

"But I need you. Please?"

"Fuck," I growl, sliding my hand around to her front and dipping my fingers into her cunt. I can't deny my woman anything, especially when she wants exactly what I want.

Circling her hard, pulsing clit with my middle finger, I rock us back and forth, grinding my dick into her juicy ass and spurting precum all over those round cheeks. When her movements become jerky, I thrust two fingers inside of her tight little channel and press the heel of my palm against her bundle of nerves.

Delaney whimpers and comes so sweetly for me, filling up my hand with her release. Only when she's nice and wet and relaxed for me do I grab her top leg and drape it over mine, opening her up for me. I tease her little entrance with the head of my cock, thrusting just inside of her and testing to see if she's lying about how sore she is.

"Jesus," I mutter. Her pussy walls pulse around the tip of my dick, massaging me and making my balls draw up tight.

That's it. My control snaps.

I thrust inside of her and groan into the back of her neck, sucking the tender skin I find there while pounding into the soft skin between her thighs. My senses are flooded with all things Delaney; her hot little pussy wrapped around my cock, her citrus scent mixed with her musky-sweet arousal, her salty sweat on my tongue, her jagged breaths and broken moans filling the air around us.

But nothing compares to seeing her surrender to her pleasure, letting go of every-fucking-thing and allowing herself to succumb to her orgasm. I fuck her through it, needing more. Needing everything.

She keeps coming, her pussy snapping around me as I bring her up and over again and again. Before her last orgasm is done, I pull out and roll her onto her back, pounding into that pretty pink pussy over and over.

"Ohmygod, I can't, I can't…" She shakes and moans for me, her entire body like a damn livewire, sparking and jerking each time I hit the end of her.

Delaney wraps her legs around me, hooking her ankles behind my back and clinging to me while I tear into her savagely.

"You can, baby, you can take it. Come for me again, one more time," I demand.

I grip her ass in a punishing hold, stroking into her roughly. Driving deeper. Hitting higher. Tilting her hips so I can scrape my cock high and hard, all the way up in the front. She moans and stretches as her head thrashes from side to side and her back arcs. Her toes curl and her fingers scrape viciously down my back until they dig into my ass. She claws and convulses and rocks her hips against me, coming with a furious, frantic energy that mirrors my own.

I roar and bite down on the top of her left breast, leaving my mark as I explode inside of her. We come together for an eternity, clinging to each other and gasping for air as our pleasure crests and then drops us back down to earth.

Rolling onto my back, I drape Delaney over my chest and kiss her sweaty temple before tucking her head under my chin. My fingers glide along her spine in calming strokes, soothing her trembling body and covering her with my strength.

"You okay, little siren?" I murmur into her beautifully untamed hair.

"So good," she mumbles, making me smirk.

"Me too."

Delaney sighs contentedly and wraps her arms around my torso, hugging me close. It's on the tip of my tongue to tell her I love her, but I can't quite get the words out. Guilt and shame grip my heart, and a picture of my parents and sister flashes through my mind.

I don't deserve happiness.

My bum leg spasms, and I clench my teeth through the pain, hating my body's betrayal. I'm a broken man, inside and out. Too fucked up for someone with tinkling laughter and beautiful, vulnerable eyes.

"Alister?" Delaney murmurs, lifting her head to look me in the eye. "Are you okay?"

"Fine," I grit out as my left leg twitches.

Delaney pulls the sheet down before I can stop her. She's seen me naked several times now, but she hasn't mentioned anything about my scar. I suppose it's faded over the years, but it will always be a hideous mark on my flesh. On my fucking soul.

"Alister," she whispers, her fingers hoving over the jagged, four-inch scar on my thigh. When she looks up, tears glisten in her multi-colored eyes. *Over me?* "Does it hurt?"

"Sometimes," I respond, trying not to roar as another spasm shoots pain down my leg. "Nerve damage. Muscle damage." I swallow down the lump in my throat, not wanting to tell her the rest. Not wanting her to know how many lives I lost in the process of getting that wound.

Delaney nods her head, though I know she still has questions. Thankfully, she seems to understand how difficult it is for me to talk about. She's got some secrets of her own that I can't pry out of her.

The little siren shocks me by leaning over and placing the lightest kiss just above my scar. She trails her lips down the marred flesh, loving me, comforting me in the most intimate way possible.

I'm broken open before this angel of light. She's wrecked me for all time. How did I survive this long without her by my side?

I reach out and comb my fingers through Delaney's hair before cupping the back of her neck and guiding her to look at me. What I see in her calico eyes blows me away. My sweet girl is devastated over whatever hurt me. She might not feel the same way once I give her my full story. But, if I want the truth from my girl, then I owe her my truth as well.

"Seven years ago," I start, my voice rough with emotion. "I was in the military. My unit was out on a mission overseas when we were ambushed." I close my eyes against the memory of that night. "We were hunkered down in our tents, laying low until morning. It was me and one other guy on watch while everyone else got some shut-eye."

I take a deep breath, bracing myself for the next part.

Delany curls up against me, resting her head on my shoulder while tracing patterns on my chest with her fingers. I wrap an arm around her waist, pulling her even closer.

"I didn't see the drone until it was too late. The first bomb dropped, and all hell broke loose."

"Oh, Alister," Delany gasps, her palm covering my heart. I place my hand over hers, keeping it there while I crack myself open.

"One after another, bombs dropped on our camp. Between shooting the drones down, ducking for cover, and trying to get as many soldiers out as possible, I somehow got a thick piece of metal shrapnel stuck in my leg. Didn't notice it until I collapsed from blood loss."

Delaney clings to me, her tears wetting the side of my neck where her face is buried. "That must have been terrifying," she whispers.

"Fear was nothing compared to the shame," I mutter.

"Shame? Alister, it wasn't your fault."

"Tell that to the three men who lost their lives that night."

"They died tragically, yes, but also heroically. They served their country well. I have no doubt you torture yourself every day about wanting to trade places."

I grunt because she's right. She already knows me so well. Too bad I'm not done airing my dirty laundry yet. "Even so, there's more."

Delaney peers up at me, encouraging me to continue.

God, she's looking at me like I'm some hero, but that couldn't be further from the truth. "I woke up a week later to doctors telling me I'd had two surgeries on my leg and I'd need to be in physical therapy for six months. My commanding officer was in the room when I came to, and I knew she had bad news for me as well."

I pause, gathering my thoughts. Delaney leans back on the pillows, then guides my head down so I'm resting on her chest. She combs her fingers through my hair, trailing them down my neck and back before reversing their path. I wrap my arms around her and slide my leg in between hers, wanting to be tangled up in my woman. She makes everything better, even the most painful memories.

"My parents and younger sister died in a house fire," I whisper, barely getting the words out. I haven't said that out loud in years. Maybe ever. "I wasn't there. I should have been there. I couldn't save them, I couldn't save the men who were bombed, I could hardly fucking function myself most days."

"Oh, my god," she whispers, clasping a hand over her mouth. "I'm so sorry."

I sit up, suddenly aware of how unworthy I am to be in Delaney's presence. My little siren follows me, wrapping herself around my back and holding me close. I relax and lean into her touch.

"That still wasn't your fault. You couldn't be everywhere at once. You were wounded! You could have died."

"Some days, I wish I did."

"But you survived," she says softly.

"Like that did anyone any good," I scoff.

Delaney pinches my side, surprisingly hard, then turns me so we're face to face. We're both still naked, and I can't help my hungry gaze from roaming up and down her bare body.

"Eyes up here, mister," she snaps. So damn adorable, even when I'm falling apart right in front of her. "You surviving sure did *me* a lot of good," she huffs out.

I nod, even managing a smile as I kiss her forehead. "You're right," I concede, my heart swelling up in my chest. What if I wasn't here when the little siren washed up on shore?

"I know," Delaney says with a cheeky grin. Her brow furrows as her features turn somber. "I'm so sorry you went through all of that. I can't imagine what the last few years have been like. Have you been out here all alone ever since?"

I nod, looking away from her.

"Alister..."

I shrug, not wanting to admit to her or myself how lonely I've been.

Delaney takes a deep breath, puffing out her cheeks as she blows it out. She flops back down on the pillows, and I watch her generous breasts bounce. When I look up, her eyes are narrowed on me, though a smirk curls up the corner of her lips.

I lay down next to her, needing to be closer. My girl is silent for long moments, and I wonder what she's thinking. I can't believe she was so understanding, so forgiving of my past. I know I have a lot of healing left to do, but for the first time since everything went down, I can see the light at the end of the tunnel. I *want* to get better. I want to be the best version of myself so I can love Delaney the way she deserves.

"My brothers got tangled up with the Romanos," Delaney murmurs.

I nod, not wanting to say anything and spook her before she tells me the rest of her story.

"I was working on a plan to leave, to get out from their controlling household. Remember I told you I was a waitress working overnights?" She waits for my nod. "My brothers didn't know about it. I was saving up for my own place. That night, though..." She pauses, swallowing thickly.

I tighten my hold on her. "I've got you, baby."

"I was sneaking back into the house, but I saw my brothers were up and had company. Instead of going in the back door, I tried the kitchen window, but I was grabbed by some mafia goon and dragged inside."

I growl, already picturing my fist going through that fucker's face.

"Save your growls until the end, please," Delaney deadpans.

I try to smile, but I can't. Not with all the red clouding my vision.

"Anyway, back to my brothers. They were meeting with a guy named Angelo, who is some high-ranking captain or something. Long story short, my brothers gave me up to the mob, but they didn't want me. Too fat, Angelo said. But I knew too much, so I had to be silenced."

"Sold you? Too fat? Jesus fucking..." My words fade into a growl. "Do you remember how you ended up in the ocean?"

Delaney closes her eyes, nodding slowly. "I passed out while I was at home. I have flashes of memories here and there of being on a boat. Cold, so cold. Water and wind and constant rocking back and forth. I fell off the boat, and my brother, Derek, just... left me. Said it would be better if I was dead, but if I manage to swim away, I should disappear for good. I floated in the dark waves, surrounded by nothing. Until you."

My heart races in my chest, pumping adrenaline through every cell, every muscle in my body. I'm ready to tear a motherfucker's head off. No way will this sin go unpunished.

"But I'm here now," she whispers, soothing her hand up and down my chest before resting it on my pounding heart. "And you're here. That's all that matters. We have each other now. Right?"

The vulnerability in her voice brings me back from the edge. There will be time for retribution, but for now, Delaney needs to see a gentler side of me. One I only seem to have around her.

"We have each other," I confirm, kissing her nose and cheeks.

I reach down and pull the covers over us, encouraging her to snuggle up next to me. We hold each other for an eternity, our hearts beating together as one.

Chapter 9

Delaney

I dry and put away the last of the dishes from breakfast, humming to myself as I waltz around the kitchen.

Ever since Alister and I shared our painful secrets, I've been light and bubbly. I feel like I could spread my wings and soar through the heavens. I'm free, and I'm right where I belong. With Alister.

I thought I was protecting the man who saved me by keeping my family history out of the picture. Seeing him break his heart open for me and tell me about his scars, both inside and out, jarred something deep in my core. This is love. Sharing your partner's burdens, holding them through the pain, and reminding them they're safe and they survived so they could be right here.

It was so healing, so life-giving, that I knew I had to tell Alister everything about me. I wanted to heal with him, to give him the chance to pick up my broken pieces too.

Today marks two weeks with my gentle giant, though it feels like we've been together forever. We've fallen into a routine of getting up early and watching the sunrise. We make breakfast together and either eat on the wrap-around deck upstairs or at the table if it's too chilly. I clean up while Alister checks on things and does the rounds, as he calls it.

I aim to have lunch ready around twelve-thirty every day, and then we go outside and work on things together. I've been helping Alister repair the stairs this week. He said he neglected them for too long, but it was the new number one priority on the island. I didn't ask him why, but I have a sneaking suspicion those stairs were not very useful when he had to carry me up from the shore.

At night, we cook, read, play games, and typically end up in bed, wrapped around each other for hours. Basically, life is perfect.

I shove away the needling thought in the back of my mind that the other shoe is going to drop at some point. Alister will get tired of me or I'll need to run to the mainland to get something and be recognized by the Romanos.

I know I need to have another talk with Alister about the future, but things are so good right now. Besides, what options do we have?

As if my thoughts conjured him into being, I hear Alister charging up the stairs. Seconds later, he bursts into the loft and beelines straight for me. I don't have time to react before he lifts me in the air and seals his lips over mine.

I welcome his kiss, wrapping my legs around his hips and holding on as he ravishes me.

"Missed you," he breathes out, resting his forehead on mine.

"It's been two hours," I say with a smile.

"Two hours too long," he grunts, kissing me again.

I giggle, breaking the kiss. Alister nips at my neck, and I squirm in his arms, hopping down and playfully pushing him away.

My gentle giant scoops me up in his arms and carries me over to the couch, sitting down with me on his lap. I beam up at him, still in awe that this man wants me. That he finds me sexy and addictive.

"So, I need to talk to you about something," he says.

I tense at his words, my stomach plummeting to my feet. Hello, other shoe. Thanks for dropping in. "Okay..." I say with more confidence than I feel.

"I have an old military buddy, Emmitt, who has a good chunk of land down in Texas. Comes from a long line of ranchers, and the place was left to him after his folks passed."

I nod, trying to follow along. What does this have to do with anything?

"He's still on active duty at the moment, but he's back on leave. I called him up this morning and asked about helping out around the ranch."

"Oh." I blink rapidly, hoping to stem the tears trying to burst free. He's leaving me.

"Yeah," Alister continues unfazed. "It's hard work, but so is keeping up this lighthouse. I figured a change of scenery would be good. I can sell this place and get a good amount of money to build something close to the ranch."

Did I read him all wrong? Was I hallucinating all the stuff he said about forever?

"Uh-huh," I respond, trying with all my might not to burst into tears. How is he being so nonchalant about this?

"Well, what do you think?" he asks.

I can't look at him.

"Sounds like you got it all figured out!" I say with all the fake happiness I can muster.

I scramble away from him, but Alister curls his hands around my hips and plops me right back down on his lap. I glare at him, setting my jaw. He wants to break up with me? Fine.

"Delaney..."

"I don't have much in the way of luggage," I attempt to joke. "So I should be out of your hair pretty quickly. If you could arrange a boat or something for me to get back to the mainland, that would be helpful. I'll just–"

"What the hell are you talking about?" Alister growls.

I glare at him. Why doesn't he understand he's breaking my heart?

"You're moving, right? So, no more roommates. No more us."

"Wait, what?"

"What, what?" I huff. "We're over, right? That's what you're trying to say."

"We're... over..."

"Yeah, I got that loud and clear. Now, will you let me go?"

"Never," he growls, standing up from the couch.

I try wiggling out of his embrace, but he turns and lays me down on the couch, climbing over me and caging me in with an arm on either side of my head.

"I'm fucking this all up," he mutters, shaking his head.

Even though this man is ripping my heart out, I hate seeing him like this. I cup his face, wanting to comfort him somehow.

Brown eyes lock onto mine, and I can see every unspoken emotion swirling in their depths. God, I'm going to miss him.

"I'm not leaving you," he finally whispers. "I'm trying to whisk you off your feet."

I give him a questioning look. "Well, I'm off my feet..."

Alister grunts and shakes his head again. "I mean, I want... I wanted to ask if you..." He takes a deep breath, his chest brushing against mine as oxygen fills his lungs. "Will you come with me? Start a new life away from your brothers and the Romanos? Away from our past? Oh, and marry me. That's the most important part."

I blink a few times, my heart stopping and then kicking into overdrive. Did I just hear him correctly? "What?"

"What, what?" he responds with a grin.

"Um, what to all of it! Are you serious?"

"Most of the time, yes."

I swat his chest, then fist his shirt, pulling him closer. "You want to keep me?"

"Delaney," he murmurs, kissing my forehead. "Always. Forever. I thought I already told you that, but I'll have to do a better job of reminding you."

I nod, making Alister smile.

He kisses the tip of my nose before continuing. "I guess I skipped over the proposal part," he says, sitting up. He pulls me up with him, adjusting us so I'm tucked into his side. "Delaney, my sweet, tempting little siren. I don't know what the hell I did to deserve your light and goodness, but it would be my honor to love you for the rest of our lives. Will you let me?"

Tears trail down my cheeks as I nod my head. "Yes," I whisper. "I love you, Alister. Thank you for saving me, for protecting me, for giving me what I needed even when I didn't know what that was."

"Baby, don't cry. We don't have to go to Texas, it was just an option. I have other friends. I think. Theo lives in New York, so that might not be the best route, but..."

"I don't care where we are," I say with a laugh. "I just want to be with you. Always."

"Then that's what you'll get, sweet girl."

"Promise?" I whisper, tipping my head up so our lips are inches apart.

"With all my heart and soul," he murmurs, closing the distance between us.

I taste promises of forever on his tongue as I fall into his embrace. I could live anywhere with this man as long as he keeps kissing me like this. In fact, I plan to do just that.

Epilogue

Alister

I pound the fence post into the ground with a final strike of the mallet and wipe the sweat from my brow. Looking over the ranch, a sense of pride settles deep in my chest. It's been happening more and more lately, and I know it's all thanks to my incredible wife.

When Delaney and I showed up here six years ago, there was a lot of work that needed to be done. Not only had the ranch been left in disarray for years, but there was a bit of a miscommunication about property lines with the neighbor.

Emmitt made it his personal responsibility to handle the problem. He ended up marrying it instead.

I scan the area for Delaney, my eyes finally resting on her hourglass figure as she walks through the garden on the east side of the property. Our kids walk alongside her, hand in hand. Camilla, our five-year-old, is very protective of her younger brother, Sam. He just turned three, and he adores following her around.

We've had our ups and downs over the years, but we're solid. I choose Delaney over everything, and she chooses me. Even when one of her brothers popped up on the scene again a few years ago. Derek.

Emmitt got a call from a guy who was inquiring about Delaney, and he told me about it right away. Derek let me know that his older brothers, Tim and Patrick, were out of the picture. He didn't spell it out for me, but I knew what he meant.

While I was glad to hear of Tim and Patrick's demise, I still wanted to reach through the phone and choke Derek. He left my woman for dead. That shit is inexcusable.

Emmitt and Theo helped me track Derek down. I paid him a visit that he won't soon forget. I didn't kill the fucker, but he was clinging to life by the time I was done.

Shaking my head of those thoughts, I take a look at the fence I've been working on all morning, then back at my wife, trying to decide if I have a few minutes to go over and see her. Who am I kidding? I always have time for my family, and I know Emmitt would understand.

Dusting my hands off on my jeans, I make my way toward Delaney and our girls. She's in a light blue sundress today, her black hair swept to the side in an elegant bun. She laughs at something Camilla said, then turns to look at me over her shoulder.

Goddamn, I'll never get tired of her smile. Her eyes always sparkle more blue than brown whenever she sees me walk into a room. I know I'm just as cheesy as she is, and I don't give a single fuck who knows it.

"Hi, baby," I say before spinning her around and dipping her low. She giggles, the tinkling sound filling me up and giving me life. Before she can say anything, I give her a swoon-worthy kiss, only pulling back when our kids start complaining.

"Daddy! Leave Mom alone. Look at my flowers!" Camilla exclaims, tugging at my shirt sleeve.

"Flowers!" Sam echoes, tugging on my other sleeve.

Delaney smiles at me, and I give her one last kiss before setting her upright on her feet. I scoop Sam up, placing him on my shoulders. He grabs my ears to steady himself, squealing with delight.

Wrapping my arm around my wife, I tuck her into my side, then hold my hand out for Camilla to take. She squeezes my fingers and leads us toward her little patch of garden.

My daughter chatters away, telling me all about the seeds she planted and how well she's been keeping up with watering them. I nod and smile, though I have no idea what she's talking about. I stick to the manual labor around here. Delaney takes care of delicate, precious things, like flowers. It fits us pretty well.

Both of our kids have shown a love for gardening. One of the first things Delaney and I did when we moved out here was to landscape the place and designate garden areas. We installed raised garden beds for the fruits and veggies and selected a mixture of bushes, trees, flowers, and other fauna to fill out the space.

Last year, Camilla got her very own plot of land for her birthday. She was over the moon about it and has taken her new responsibility seriously.

Sam is a little too young to garden, but my boy sure likes playing in the dirt. He wiggles on my shoulders, and I let him down, grinning when he plops down on the ground and shoves his hands in the dirt pile in front of him.

"Are you going to be giving him a bath tonight?" Delaney asks as she eyes Sam and his messy hands and clothes.

"Sure," I answer easily. "Then I can give you a bath," I murmur into the shell of her ear.

Delaney leans further into me as I kiss the sensitive spot just beneath her ear. "I think I like showers better," she muses. "More... possibilities."

I groan and nuzzle into the side of her neck, picturing my gorgeous wife naked and dripping wet. "You're killing me here. I still have a whole afternoon on the ranch."

Delaney shrugs, giving me the sexiest little smirk. "Better hurry up, then."

I lean in and kiss her, because how could I not? "I love you, little siren," I whisper.

"Love you too, gentle giant."

I smile, brushing my nose against hers. This woman. I may have taken her in and given her shelter when she needed it, but she's the one who saved me. It's my deepest honor and greatest joy to spend the rest of my life protecting her precious light.

Connect with me!

Check out my website, cameronhart.net[1], for sneak previews on my latest projects.

Follow me on social media:

Facebook Page - facebook.com/cameronhartauthor
    Instagram - instagram.com/cameron.hart.author
    TikTok - tiktok.com/@author.cameron.hart
    Goodreads - goodreads.com/16081533.Cameron_Hart
    Bookbub - bookbub.com/authors/cameron-hart

---

1. https://cameronhart.net/

www.ingramcontent.com/pod-product-compliance
Lightning Source LLC
Chambersburg PA
CBHW031137160726

47987CB00026B/1214